To my Dad
AB

For John and Mandi
with much love
VF

HODDER CHILDREN'S BOOKS

First published in Great Britain in 1995 by Hodder Children's Books
This edition published in 2016 by Hodder and Stoughton

33 34 35 36 37 38 39 40

Text copyright © Vivian French, 1995
Illustrations copyright © Alison Bartlett, 1995

A CIP catalogue record for this book is available from the British Library.

ISBN 978-0-340-63479-0

Printed in China

Hodder Children's Books
An imprint of
Hachette Children's Group
Part of Hodder and Stoughton
Carmelite House
50 Victoria Embankment
London EC4Y 0DZ

An Hachette UK Company
www.hachette.co.uk
www.hachettechildrens.co.uk

Oliver's Vegetables

Vivian French

Illustrated by
AIison BartIett

h
Hodder
Children's
Books

"Finish up, Oliver," said his mum,
"or we'll miss the bus."
"Can't we walk to Grandpa's house?"
asked Oliver.
"No," said his mother. "It's too far.
Hurry up!"

The best thing about Grandpa's house was the wonderful garden.
"I grow all my own vegetables," Grandpa said proudly.

"I don't eat vegetables," Oliver told Grandpa.
"I only eat chips."
"If you want chips," said Grandpa, "you must find
the potatoes. If you find something else, you eat that
and no complaints. Is it a bargain?"

Oliver ran round the garden, but he couldn't see any potatoes.
"They must be hiding," he said, and pulled at the nearest leaves.
"Carrots," said Grandpa. "Just the thing for Monday lunch."
Oliver ate his first carrots for lunch.

Oliver took a long time making up his
mind on Tuesday. Gran and Grandpa
came to watch him.
"Those crinkly leaves are pretty,"
he said at last. "Are the potatoes there?"
"Spinach," said Grandpa.
They had spinach for supper.
"That was good,"
said Oliver.

On Wednesday Oliver got up early.
"Potatoes are very important," he said, "so they
must have big leaves. *HERE THEY ARE!*"
Grandpa smiled. "That's rhubarb."
They had rhubarb pie that evening.
"That was very good," said Oliver.

It rained on Thursday. When it stopped, Oliver hurried outside. "Have you found the potatoes?" Grandpa asked.
"No," said Oliver. "I've found slugs and snails. Are they eating my potatoes?"
Grandpa shook his head. "That's cabbage."
Oliver had two helpings.
"Very, very good," he said.

On Friday Oliver was sure that he had found the
potatoes. When he pulled at the leaves, up came
some beetroot. That night Oliver ate all
of his beetroot salad.
"Very, very, very good," he said.

On Saturday Oliver
played football.
The ball landed
in a tangle
of sticks and leaves.
Oliver was sure the
potatoes weren't there,
and Grandpa nodded.
"Peas," he said.
Oliver had three helpings
of pea soup that evening.
"Was that good?"
asked Grandpa.
"No," said Oliver,
"it was delicious!"

Oliver rushed into the garden on Sunday.
"HERE THEY ARE!"
"How did you know?" asked Grandpa.
"They were the only things left," said Oliver.

"Can we have chips now?" Oliver asked.
"You scrub the potatoes," said Gran,
"and I'll peel them. Grandpa
can cut them up."

Oliver, Gran and Grandpa sat down to eat.
The door opened and in walked Oliver's mother.
She saw the plate of chips.
"Oh dear. I did hope Oliver would eat
something different while he was here," she said.
Oliver and Grandpa looked at each other.
His mother stared as they laughed and
laughed and laughed.